My House

Byron Barton

Greenwillow Books
An Imprint of HarperCollins Publishers

Library of Congress Cataloging-in-Publication Data
Barton, Byron, author, illustrator. My house / written and illustrated by Byron Barton.
  pages cm   "Greenwillow Books."
Summary: "Jim the cat describes his favorite places inside and outside his house"—
Provided by publisher.
ISBN 978-0-06-233703-0 (trade ed.)
(1. Cats—Fiction. 2. Dwellings—Fiction.) I. Title. PZ7.B2848Myh 2016 (E)—dc23 2015010295
First Edition 16 17 18 19 20 SCP 10 9 8 7 6 5 4 3 2 1

 Greenwillow Books

To Tubby

I am Jim.

This is
my house.

This is the roof of my house.

These are windows.

This is the door.

This is the inside
of my house.

This is my
living room.

This is
the kitchen.

Upstairs
is the
bedroom.

This is my bed.

This is the
bathroom.

This is my litter box.

I hear
a noise
downstairs.

It is Jane.

Jane makes
my dinner.

I like my house.

I like my tree.

I like my home. Meow.